OTHER YEARLING BOOKS
BY PATRICIA REILLY GIFF YOU WILL ENJOY:

THE MYSTERY OF THE BLUE RING
THE RIDDLE OF THE RED PURSE
THE SECRET AT THE POLK STREET SCHOOL
THE POWDER PUFF PUZZLE
THE BEAST IN MS. ROONEY'S ROOM
FISH FACE
THE CANDY CORN CONTEST
IN THE DINOSAUR'S PAW
THE VALENTINE STAR
LAZY LIONS, LUCKY LAMBS
SNAGGLE DOODLES
PURPLE CLIMBING DAYS
SAY "CHEESE"
SUNNY-SIDE UP
PICKLE PUSS

YEARLING BOOKS/YOUNG YEARLINGS/YEARLING CLASSICS are designed especially to entertain and enlighten young people. Patricia Reilly Giff, consultant to this series, received her bachelor's degree from Marymount College and a master's degree in history from St. John's University. She holds a Professional Diploma in Reading and a Doctorate of Humane Letters from Hofstra University. She was a teacher and reading consultant for many years, and is the author of numerous books for young readers.

For a complete listing of all Yearling titles,
write to Dell Readers Service,
P.O. Box 1045, South Holland, IL 60473.

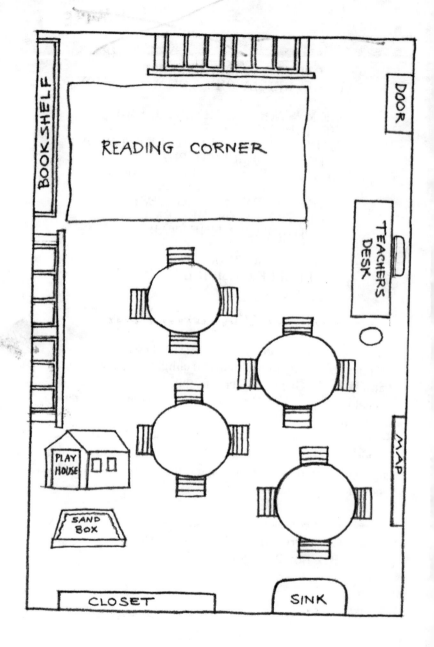

New Kids
2
at the Polk Street School

Fancy Feet

Patricia Reilly Giff

Illustrated by Blanche Sims

A YOUNG YEARLING BOOK

Published by
Dell Publishing
a division of
Bantam Doubleday Dell Publishing Group, Inc.
1540 Broadway
New York, New York 10036

Thank you to Flo Gatsche

ISBN: 0-440-40086-4

Printed in the United States of America

October 1988

10 9

WES

For Sister Immaculata, C.S.J.

CHAPTER

1

Stacy was a bird.

She held out her arms.

She flew around the schoolyard. "Watch out."

No one in the class listened.

They were yelling too.

It was recess.

Stacy saw her friend Jiwon. "Honk, honk, Gee," she said.

Jiwon was hopping around. "I'm a kangaroo," she called.

Out of the corner of her eye Stacy saw A.J.

He was down on his hands and knees. He was making noises.

Stacy flew a little closer.

A.J. put his head down. He swung one arm in front of him.

"Are you an elephant?" Stacy asked.

"Bra-a-ay," A.J. said in a deep voice.

"I thought so," Stacy said. She said it over her shoulder.

She flew around him.

"Watch out, Stacy," Mrs. Zachary called.

It was too late.

Stacy flew into Eddie.

Eddie went down hard.

So did Stacy.

"Hey," Eddie said. He looked at his jeans. "A hole."

Stacy held up her knee. "Hey. Blood."

Mrs. Zachary came over.

She helped Stacy up.

"Oh, dear," she said.

She helped Eddie up too.

"Band-Aids in my desk," she said. "And you can get a nice drink of water, Stacy. You'll feel better in a few minutes."

Stacy stood up. She felt better right now.

She didn't tell Mrs. Zachary that.

Mrs. Zachary might not let her get Band-Aids.

She might not let her get a nice drink of water.

Stacy marched into school with Eddie.

She made believe she was limping.

She limped a lot.

She hoped someone would say, "Poor Stacy."

Nobody did though.

She looked back.

A.J. was crawling around again.

Jiwon was hopping.

"What's Patty doing?" Eddie asked.

Stacy raised one shoulder. "I don't know."

"I think she's a snake," Eddie said.

Stacy watched Patty.

She was crawling on the ground.

"Maybe she's a worm," Stacy said.

She started to run.

She flew down the hall.

"Honk," she said.

Eddie put his finger on his lips.

"Mrs. Zachary says don't talk in the hall."

Stacy honked again. A little honk.

Sometimes Eddie was a pain, she thought.

Ms. Rooney poked her head out of 113. "Is someone making noise out here?"

Stacy slowed down.

She began to limp again.

"We're hurt," she said. "I was a bird."

"I was a water buffalo," said Eddie.

"Is that what a water buffalo looks like?" Stacy asked.

Ms. Rooney smiled at them.

She closed her door.

Stacy and Eddie went into their room.

They looked at Mrs. Zachary's desk.

A bunch of things were on top. Pencils and scissors and a magic marker. Books and two Band-Aids with green dots.

A piece of gold paper with a shiny *S*.

Stacy smiled.

Now she knew a secret.

It was going to be *S* week.

Stacy picked up the two Band-Aids.

She began to pull one open.

Eddie sat on the floor.

He looked at his jeans. "I could put a Band-Aid on my knee. You wouldn't even see the hole."

Stacy looked down. "I need them for my knee."

"You don't need both." He made a face. "That sore is smaller than an ant. A little tiny ant."

"It is not." She slapped a Band-Aid on her knee. It went straight up and down.

She slapped the other one on sideways.

"One goes one way," she said. "The other goes the other way."

Eddie stuck out his lip. "Let's go."

"I wonder what's in Mrs. Zachary's drawer," Stacy said.

"My mother says don't open anyone's dresser drawers," Eddie said.

"Does this look like a dresser?" Stacy honked. "This is a desk."

She started to open it.

"Let's get out of here," Eddie said. "I don't want to be in trouble."

Stacy took a breath. "Hey. Look."

He tiptoed over.

"A million dollars," Stacy said.

"Wow," said Eddie.

"Mrs. Zachary is rich," said Stacy.

They could hear the class coming.

Stacy slammed the drawer shut.

Mrs. Zachary rich.

She couldn't believe it.

The class marched in.

Stacy went to her seat.

Then she remembered.

She had forgotten her nice drink of water.

She raised her hand.

CHAPTER

2

Stacy wiped her mouth.

She slid into her seat.

"We start a new letter today," said Mrs. Zachary.

"Sss," Stacy hissed.

"No more *M*?" Jiwon asked.

"Sss," Stacy said again.

"We have a special letter this week," said Mrs. Zachary.

Stacy smiled. A big smile. She showed all her teeth.

She knew why *S* was special.

S was the start of her name.

"Who can guess . . ." Mrs. Zachary began.

Stacy raised her hand.

She raised it high in the air.

She kept making *S* sounds.

She wanted Mrs. Zachary to know she had the right answer.

Jiwon's hand was up too.

So were Patty's and A.J.'s.

Eddie wasn't listening. He had his head under the table.

He was eating his snack.

Stacy could smell it.

It was peanut butter.

That's what Eddie had every day.

"All right," said Mrs. Zachary. "You may guess, Eddie."

"Five," he said.

Mrs. Zachary shook her head. "That's a number. We're doing letters."

Stacy laughed a little.

She didn't laugh much though.

She liked Eddie.

She didn't want to hurt his feelings.

Maybe he was going to be her husband someday.

"Here comes the bride," Stacy

hummed under her breath. "All dressed in green."

Jiwon leaned over to listen.

"When Jiwon saw her . . ." Stacy sang softly, "she started to scream."

Jiwon laughed.

Stacy laughed too.

Mrs. Zachary clapped her hands.

Eddie snapped up his head.

He had peanut butter all over his face.

Patty called out. "Is it X?"

Mrs. Zachary smiled. "X is a nice letter." She shook her head. "But that's not the one."

Stacy knelt up on her chair. She said, "Ssss."

She kept saying it.

It sounded as if a firecracker were in the room.

"Boom," Stacy said.

"Stacy," said Mrs. Zachary. "Please sit down."

Stacy slid down.

Mrs. Zachary didn't sound very friendly, she thought.

She sighed. She was tired of waiting for Mrs. Zachary to call on her.

Eddie stood up.

He didn't wait for Mrs. Zachary to call on him.

"It's *S*," he told Mrs. Zachary.

"No fair," said Stacy.

"Right, Edward," Mrs. Zachary said. "What a good guess."

Stacy put her fingers in her mouth. She pulled her lips open wide.

She stuck out her tongue.

It was her best witch face.

She'd never marry him now. Eddie wasn't even looking at her though. He was smiling.

He was glad he was right.

"I don't think Eddie was guessing," Stacy said.

But Mrs. Zachary didn't hear her.

She held up the gold paper with the

big green *S*. "Do you know why this letter is special?"

Stacy waved her hand around. "It says my name."

"Yes, indeed," said Mrs. Zachary. "Ssss Stacy." She said it with her teeth sticking out.

Stacy loved Mrs. Zachary's big teeth. She stuck her teeth out a little too. "Yes, indeed," she told the class.

Mrs. Zachary raised her eyebrows. "Let's all make the *S* sound."

The class said *S*.

Stacy said it the loudest.

It was her own letter.

"Wonderful," said Mrs. Zachary. She looked around at the class. "Sit up tall. Here comes a surprise."

Stacy sat up tall. Taller than Jiwon. Much taller than Eddie.

Almost as tall as Patty.

Mrs. Zachary opened her desk drawer. She took out a bunch of dollars.

Millions of them.

"Wow," yelled A.J.

"Mrs. Zachary is rich," Stacy said. "I knew it."

Then she closed her mouth.

She didn't want Mrs. Zachary to know she had seen that money before.

"We're going to have a store," said Mrs. Zachary.

"S for store," said Jiwon.

"Yes, indeed," said Mrs. Zachary.

"Yes, indeed," said Stacy.

"It will be right here," said Mrs. Zachary. "In our room."

Stacy raised her hand.

She wanted to know what she could buy.

She had eleven cents.

It was for sweeping the garage.

Then she remembered.

She had spent eight cents.

Teeny Tiny Bubble Gum was on sale.

Emily had said it was no good.

Emily was right.

It didn't even make bubbles.

She remembered something else.

The rest of her money was lost somewhere.

Stacy put her hand down.

She couldn't buy anything.

Not one thing.

CHAPTER
3

Stacy pulled everything out of her toy chest.

"Look-look-looking," she sang to herself. "What's no-no-good?"

She held up her green yo-yo.

The string was missing.

It was worse than no good.

It was broken.

Mrs. Zachary had said not to bring anything broken.

She had said it in her "I mean it" voice.

Stacy threw the yo-yo back in the toy chest.

Her mother came to the door. "What a mess."

"Guess what?" Stacy said. "The best thing."

Her mother sat down with her. "What?"

Stacy took a breath. "We're going to have a store. We have to bring something. Me. Jiwon. A.J. Everyone."

"Nice," said her mother.

"Yes, indeed," said Stacy.

Her mother laughed.

"Mrs. Zachary has a million dollars," said Stacy.

"I didn't know that," her mother said.

"Not real ones," said Stacy. She shook her head. "I found out they're just-for-fun money."

Stacy held up a candy necklace.

It was all stuck together.

"Yuck," she said.

"Throw that in the garbage," said her mother.

Stacy nodded. "I will."

She put it down on the floor.

"We're going to earn money," she said. "Let's say I sit up straight. I don't talk. I do a whole page of *S S S*. I get two dollars maybe. Two just-for-fun dollars."

"Great," said her mother.

"I can be good every day. I can be wonderful." She looked up. "I'll buy out the whole store."

Stacy's mother looked into the toy chest.

"Why don't you get rid of that junk?"

"I am," said Stacy. "I'm going to bring it for the store. Mrs. Zachary said it's good for us to share."

"I think so too," said her mother.

"Yes, indeed," said Stacy.

She stuck her head in the chest. "I'll buy some of Jiwon's stuff. Or A.J.'s."

Her mother laughed. "More junk."

"Good junk," said Stacy. "Different junk."

Her mother leaned over. She gave Stacy a hug. "I have to make dinner now."

She went out the door.

Stacy pulled out an old horse on a stick.

Maybe she could bring that.

She shook her head. No. It was baby stuff.

Everyone would laugh.

Just then Emily came in. She said hi to Stacy.

"We're having a store-store-store," Stacy sang.

"We had one in kindergarten too," said Emily.

She put her books on the floor.

She put her jacket on top of them.

"Now I know where everything is," Emily said.

She knelt down.

She looked in the toy chest.

"What junk," she said.

"I know," said Stacy.

"Bring something nice," said Emily.

"I'm trying," Stacy said. "I just can't find anything."

Emily looked around the room.

Stacy looked too.

"How about that bank?" Emily asked.

"My bunny bank? My favorite old bunny bank?"

"Yes. That would be good."

Stacy stuck out her lip. "I love that bank. I got it for my birthday."

Emily didn't say anything.

"Besides," Stacy said. "It has fifty cents in it. I can't get it out."

Emily sat back. "Hey. What am I kneeling on?"

"I think it's a candy necklace," said Stacy.

"Gross," Emily said. "Disgusting."

She rubbed at her knee.

Stacy leaned over. "It'll come off. Don't worry."

Emily scratched a little harder.

"What did you bring, old Emily?" Stacy asked.

"What?"

"To the store."

Emily thought. "A book, I think. Yes. A book."

"That's what I'm bringing," said Stacy. "Yes, indeed."

She stood up. She went over to her bookcase.

"Those scribble-scrabble books?" Emily said. "You wrote all over them."

"I did it when I was a baby," Stacy said.

"Ha," said Emily. "You did it last summer."

Stacy looked at the books.

She had made red curlicues on the front.

Inside too.
Too bad.
She had nothing else to bring.
She'd have to bring a book.

CHAPTER
4

Stacy was standing at the easel.

It was her turn to paint.

She closed one eye.

She looked at the big white paper.

Her picture would be gorgeous.

It was going to be the Polk Street School.

She ran the brush across the paper.

Back and forth.

Up and down.

She stood back.

Now there was a red box on the paper.

It took up most of the page.

A skinny red line dripped down one side.

It dropped onto the leg of the easel.

Stacy dabbed at it.

A few red dots landed on the floor.

She put her foot over the dots.

The she checked the picture again.

She clicked her teeth.

No windows.

She had painted the whole thing red.

She put her brush in the water.

Never mind about the windows.

She'd put a flag on top. Then some grass.

No one would see there were no windows.

She looked up.

Mrs. Zachary was working on the store.

Jiwon and Patty were helping.

Stacy's book was on one shelf.

She could see the red scribble-scrabble.

Another book was on the shelf.

It was Twana's.

It was new and shiny.

Stacy clicked her teeth again.

Maybe she should have brought a shiny new book too.

Mrs. Zachary was putting more things on the shelf.

She put a pink panda on top.

It was a yucko one. It had a pushed-in nose.

"That's my panda," Eddie told her.

"Not such a hot nose," Stacy said.

"I gave it a karate chop," he said.

"Look what I brought," Jiwon told the class.

She opened a brown paper bag.

Everyone said, "Oh."

"Beautiful," said Twana.

Stacy couldn't see. She stepped around the easel.

Jiwon was holding up a pair of ladies' shoes. "My mother's," she said. "They're a little too small."

Stacy took a breath.

The shoes were gorgeous.

"I wanted to bring something nice," Jiwon said. "Something really nice to share."

"Me too," said Stacy.

"You think that scribbly book is nice?" Twana asked.

Stacy didn't answer.

Jiwon put on the shoes.

She danced around the front of the room.

Stacy kept looking at the shoes.

They were gold.

They were shiny.

They glittered on Jiwon's feet.

Stacy stood on tiptoes.

Lucky Jiwon.

The shoes had high heels.

If they were hers, she wouldn't give them away.

Never.

Stacy made believe she was dancing.

She made believe she had on the high heels.

She wanted those shoes.

She wanted them more than any-thing.

More than a million dollars.

She knocked over the red paint.

"Oops," she said.

"You're going to be in trouble," Eddie said.

"Be quiet," Stacy said.

She took a quick look at Mrs. Zachary.

Mrs. Zachary was putting a truck on a shelf.

Stacy picked up a newspaper.

She rubbed it on the paint.

The paint spread over the floor.

"Look what you did," said Twana. "You made a big mess."

Stacy made a witch face at her.

"Mrs. Zachary," Twana called. "Stacy made a mess. She made a witch face too."

Mrs. Zachary turned around.

Stacy rubbed at the red paint.

Then she started to cry.

She'd never earn any just-for-fun money.

She'd never get those shoes.

CHAPTER
5

Mrs. Zachary held up her paper. "Do it like this," she said.

She folded the paper in half.

Stacy folded hers in half too.

She put it on her desk.

The middle pointed up.

It looked like a tent.

Stacy blew on it. "I'm the wind," she said.

The tent moved a little.

Stacy poked Eddie.

"Look," she said. "It's a storm."

She made some storm noises. "Shim. Shum. Baboom."

She blew hard.

Her tent blew off her table.

Mrs. Zachary frowned. "Stacy Arrow," she said. "Pay attention."

Stacy put her eyes down.

She looked at the table.

She picked up her paper with one hand.

She didn't look at the teacher.

Mrs. Zachary would know she was sad.

But Mrs. Zachary wasn't looking at her. She was putting a big number 6 on the board.

Stacy put her hand up.

"That's me. That's my age."

"Me too," said Jiwon.

"Me too," said some other children.

Mrs. Zachary smiled.

Stacy smiled back. She smiled with her teeth.

"Let's draw six things on our paper," said Mrs. Zachary.

Stacy picked up her crayon.

She knew what to do.

She was going to draw six elephants.

Six cute elephants.

Mrs. Zachary would give her a star.

She'd give her a pile of just-for-fun money.

Stacy would race up to the store.

She'd grab the shoes. She'd bring them home.

They'd be hers forever.

Stacy bent over her paper. She did the first elephant.

Too bad she couldn't erase crayon.

It wasn't such a great elephant.

She turned her paper over. She started again.

Eddie leaned over her shoulder. "What's that?"

"An elephant, of course," Stacy said.

Eddie began to laugh. "It looks like a snake with a hat."

Stacy covered her paper. "It does not."

Eddie laughed harder.

Stacy looked at his fat cheeks.

"Stop laughing," she said.

Eddie didn't stop. He kept making he-he-he sounds.

His cheeks were red.

He had tears in his eyes.

"Look," he told Jiwon. "He. He. He. A snake. A snake with a hat."

Stacy wanted to cry.

She swung her hand around.

Whack.

She smacked Eddie hard.

Everyone looked at her.

Eddie started to cry.

Mrs. Zachary turned around.

"Stacy Arrow," she said. "No recess for you."

"No just-for-fun money either," said Twana.

Stacy stuck her lip out.

She didn't finish her elephants.

They were miserable elephants.

She just sat there.

Then everyone lined up.

"I'll be right back," Mrs. Zachary told her. "I want to bring the children to Mr. Bell."

The class marched out.

Then it was quiet.

She was all alone.

She sniffed a little.

She hated Eddie. Twana too.

She hated everyone in the world.

Almost everyone.

She didn't hate Mrs. Zachary. Mrs. Zachary had such a nice smile.

Mrs. Zachary probably hated her.

She was a terrible girl.

Stacy stood up. She went over to the store.

The gold shoes were on top.

She looked at them.

Then she stood up tall.

She reached for the shoes.

She put them on.

Perfect.

She walked around for a minute.

The heels were high. She kept turning on her ankles.

She tiptoed to the window.

Outside, everyone was playing.

She didn't care.

She'd rather dance in the shoes.

"La dee, la dee, dee," she sang.

She twirled around.

The shoes clicked.

Wonderful.

She heard footsteps.

Mrs. Zachary was coming.

She had to put the shoes back.

It was too late.

Mrs. Zachary was almost there.

Stacy looked around.

She threw the shoes in the wastebasket.

She'd get them out later.

She banged down in her seat.

She slid into her sneakers.

Her face felt hot.

She could feel her heart pounding.

She hoped Mrs. Zachary couldn't see
the shoes in the basket.

She was in enough trouble now.

CHAPTER
6

Today was Thursday.

Stacy wished it were Saturday.

She wished she didn't have to go back to school.

"What do you think jail is like?" she asked Emily.

"Watch out for cars," Emily said.

"I am." Stacy looked up at Emily. "Do you think jail is terrible?"

"I certainly do," said Emily. "No television. No candy."

"No mother and father," said Stacy.

"Hurry a little," Emily said. "I don't want to be late for school."

Stacy didn't want to hurry.

She knew she was going to jail.

The gold shoes were gone.

By now, Jim the custodian had thrown them away.

Stacy sighed.

Yesterday she had forgotten all about the shoes.

She hadn't remembered until bedtime.

Poor gold shoes.

Poor Stacy.

Mrs. Zachary had scolded her about hitting Eddie.

Stacy had to tell him she was sorry.

She had to promise not to hit people again.

No wonder she had forgotten the shoes.

All because of that pain, Eddie.

Stacy walked across the schoolyard with Emily.

Maybe she should run away.

Then she stopped. No one knew she had taken the shoes.

No one knew she had put them in the wastebasket.

"Little kids don't go to jail anyway," she told Emily.

Emily wasn't paying attention.

"Em-i-ly," she said. "Little kids don't go to jail."

Emily waved at her friend Jill. "If they do something terrible, they do."

"Oh," said Stacy. It was hard to swallow. "I didn't do anything."

She crossed her fingers.

She went to her line.

She sang to herself. "I didn't do anything, thing, thing."

Then she stopped singing.

"Yes I did, did, did," she whispered.

She went inside with the rest of her class.

She took a quick look at the waste-basket.

It was empty.

She knew it.

Then she looked at the store.

No shoes.

Just a scribble-scrabble red book.

Just a couple of trucks.

Twana's book was gone.

A.J. had bought it yesterday. He had remembered to say excuse me.

He had said it about forty-two times.

He had gotten a pile of just-for-fun money.

Stacy slid into her seat.

Mrs. Zachary was standing at Twana's table.

She was giving out beads.

Everyone would put them on strings. They were going to make gorgeous necklaces.

Mrs. Zachary came to Stacy's table.

She put a zillion beads in the middle.

Fat orange ones. Round red ones. Long, skinny blue ones.

Stacy took a red bead.

It was her favorite color.

She didn't feel like making a gorgeous necklace.

She kept thinking about the gold shoes.

Just then Jiwon pulled on Mrs. Zachary's sleeve.

"My shoes are gone," she said.

Mrs. Zachary looked up. "We didn't sell them, did we?"

Jiwon shook her head hard.

Patty came over. "I wanted those shoes. I had almost enough just-for-fun money."

"Me too," said Twana. She looked as if she were going to cry.

Stacy wanted to say something.

Her mouth was dry.

She put the red bead on the string.

She picked up a blue one.

Mrs. Zachary went over to the store.

She looked at the shelves.

"Oh, dear," she said. "What could have happened?"

"Maybe someone threw them out," Stacy said. "By accident."

"I don't think so," said Mrs. Zachary.

"I don't think so either," said Twana. "I think someone took them."

"Not me," said Stacy. She crossed her fingers.

"Not me," said A.J. He started to laugh. "I don't wear high heels."

Jiwon started to cry.

Mrs. Zachary patted her shoulder. "Don't worry. We'll find them. Let's all look hard."

Everyone ran around looking hard.

Stacy made believe she was looking too.

Twana tapped her shoulder. "Stealing Stacy. That's you."

Eddie came up behind them. "Stacy's a nice girl. She wouldn't steal anything."

Stacy looked at Eddie.

He was a good friend.

"I won't hit you anymore," Stacy said. "Really."

She wasn't such a good friend though.

Not to Eddie.

Not to Jiwon.

She swallowed. What was she going to do?

CHAPTER
7

Today was different.

Stacy didn't go to school with Emily.

She nearly didn't go to school at all.

She had coughed eleven times at breakfast.

She had tried to sneeze too.

It was hard to sneeze when you didn't have to.

"I'm sick," Stacy told her mother.

"Very, very sick. I have to stay in bed all day."

"What's the matter?" her mother asked.

"I have chicken heads."

Emily laughed. "You mean chicken pox."

"That's what I have," Stacy said.

"That's what you don't have," said her mother.

Emily got ready for school.

Stacy pulled on one sock.

"I'm going to be late," Emily said.

"Go ahead," said their mother. "Go without Stacy."

Stacy was surprised. Maybe she didn't have to go to school after all.

Her mother came into her bedroom. "What's really the matter?" she asked.

Stacy coughed once.

She could feel her eyes making tears.

"Come on," said her mother. "Tell me." She sat down on Stacy's bed.

Stacy sat on the bed too. "One. I threw away Jiwon's shoes. Two. I'm not a good sharer. Everyone is better than me. Eddie. Jiwon . . ."

Her mother shook her head. "I don't think everyone is better . . ."

Stacy shook her head up and down.

"I even brought an old scribble-scrabble book."

"Hmm," said her mother. "What can you do?"

"Stay home."

"Let's think of something else," said her mother.

Stacy watched her mother thinking.

She tried to think too.

She remembered today was Patty's birthday.

Patty's mother was bringing cupcakes.

She tried to think harder.

She hated to miss cupcakes.

Patty said they were chocolate mint.

Stacy looked at her mother. "Did you think of something?"

"Not yet," said her mother.

Stacy thought another minute. "I know what I'm going to do," she said.

"Good."

Her mother stood up. She gave Stacy a big hug. "Hurry up. Get dressed. I'll drive you to school."

Stacy threw her clothes on.

She ran out to the car.

She stopped. "I nearly forgot."

She raced back into the house.

She came back with a paper bag.

"Suppose you did something bad?" she asked her mother.

"Tell about it," her mother said. "You'll feel better."

"That's what I'm going to do," Stacy said. "Yes, indeed."

She bit her lip.

She was afraid to tell.

Stacy was the last one in school.

Everything was quiet.

She walked down the hall quietly.

Eddie was right.

You should be quiet in the hall.

She hurried into the classroom.

Mrs. Zachary looked up. "I thought

you were sick, Stacy. I'm glad you're not."

Stacy went up to Mrs. Zachary's desk.

She put down the paper bag.

"What's this?"

"It's a bank. My best birthday bank. It's for the store. It has fifty cents inside for new shoes."

Mrs. Zachary nodded. "I see."

"I told you," Twana said. "Stealing Stacy."

Eddie shook his head.

Mrs. Zachary held up her hand. "Maybe Stacy wants to tell us about it."

"I didn't steal," Stacy said. "At least I didn't mean to."

She took a breath.

She was going to tell the whole thing.

She felt better already.

Much better.

Then she was going to be as good as she could.

She was going to start saving all over again.